HOT PENNIES

SHANE SIMMONS

ISBN: 978-1-988954-03-5

Published by Eyestrain Productions
eyestrainproductions.com

"YOU DON'T WANT to go to the hospital tonight, sweetie. The emergency room's full of crazies. I'll take you in the morning."

Kurt McGowan whimpered pathetically as he soaked his fingers in a bowl of ice water his mother had prepared for him. She was determined the burns weren't serious enough to race down to the hospital at this hour. Some cream and bandages and crushed children's Aspirin would hold her boy over for the night. But Kurt was just as determined to let the full extent of his pain be known to anyone within earshot. He wanted an audience of doctors and nurses to play to, just as he had two years earlier when he was eight and had broken his wrist during a particularly splendid bike crash.

A few more whimpers, maybe a soulful moan or two, and his doting mother would crack. She always did, she always would. She knew she was an easy touch, and was trying to take steps to harden her heart. The last thing she wanted was for her son to grow up with whining as his only means of manipulation. That would make him no better than his father.

Kurt's mother resolved to hold off for another hour. Or another half hour at least. Certainly she could wait and see if he settled down in the next fifteen minutes.

● ● ●

Anyone will tell you that New Year's Eve is the worst shift of all. Hands down, flat out, no doubt about it. The number of injuries is unparalleled, as is the amount of vomit that has the janitorial staff mopping the halls straight through till morning. There's one other annual occasion, however, that runs a close second. On a bad night, it can come very close to matching the injury and vomit quota. The one pivotal difference is the culprit behind it all. Alcohol is the root cause of New Year's mayhem, but it's sugar at the core of Hallowe'en.

November 1st was still several hours away and already the emergency room was brimming, filled to overflowing with the casualties of costume parties and trick-or-treatings and savage eggings. The kids started coming in as soon as the sun went down—the accidents, the injuries, the boo-boos filled the charts in record time. It would take all night to stitch everyone back together. By the time the sun was up again, the second wave of ailing children would begin to arrive. These would be the ones who had been up half the night gorging on goodies. They would be sick or simply nauseous, coming down hard from sugar highs, and desperate for something to settle their swollen bellies. One or two might need to have their stomachs pumped if they'd been especially gluttonous.

Neil Leverault hadn't volunteered for this. He'd worked at Templeton General long enough to know better, and was a physician with enough seniority to ditch the shit shifts. But this year he'd been outmanoeuvred. A particularly hot party hosted by a particularly hot nurse had drawn doctors from all levels of the medical hierarchy like flies. Most of them had been clever enough to arrange for time off weeks in advance. Others had merely called in sick at the last minute. This ultimately left Neil holding the bag along with a few other lonely souls who had little or no interest in popular parties or nurses who knew how to fill out a set of scrubs.

Neil inspected the rows of victims in the waiting room chairs. They were staggered in a wounded-child/concerned-parent-or-guardian pattern that re-peated itself a couple of dozen times until there was standing room only. Templeton was small enough for Neil to know most of the kids by sight and most-frequent medical complaint.

Hugh Winburn was nine years old and suffered from chronic ear infections. Tonight he'd provoked a schoolmate who had dared tease him about his unimaginative clown costume. The schoolmate, dressed as an executioner complete with black mask and axe, had remained calm, even stoic, until Hugh suggested that his sister's Hallowe'en costume made her look even more like a whore than she usually did. That's when the executioner swung his halberd at him and landed a blow across Hugh's fingers. The halberd was only wood, painted silver to look like metal, and far too dull to cut anything. But it was still a solid ten pounds of lumber, and it handily crushed all four fingers that got in its way, breaking two.

Alan Jaycox was ten, and until tonight had never come to emergency with anything more serious than a bump or a scrape. Most of his hair had been scorched off an hour earlier when he thought it might be fun to toss a cherry bomb into a jack-o-lantern on his neighbour's porch. Unfortunately, the pumpkin had been lit by an oil lamp, and the whole thing went up with a deafening bang that sent flames and pulpy orange shrapnel flying up to thirty feet in all directions. Burns to Alan's scalp were only superficial. More serious burns were averted when an alert friend smothered Alan's blazing cape with his own more flame-retardant cloak.

Then there was Peter Paulson, eight and asthmatic, who had the dubious distinction of bringing an apocryphal urban legend to life by biting into an apple that really had a razor blade embedded in it. The blade had slipped neatly between his gapped front teeth and lodged itself deep into his gums as he bit down. He now sat next to his mother on one of the hard plastic waiting chairs, his mouth hanging open foolishly because he couldn't close it without causing further damage. It looked terribly painful, but the greatest injury was to Peter's pride. Unable to swallow effectively, he drooled a steady line of bloody saliva from his pulled-back lips. Peter was sure it made him look like an imbecile. He certainly felt like one for falling victim to that most legendary of Hallowe'en treat sabotages.

"How you doing, Pete?" asked Kurt McGowan as he entered the waiting room and spotted his third best friend slobbering all over himself. Kurt's mother was still at the registration desk, securing their place in line. Now that he was at the hospital, and away from the immediate presence of his mom, Kurt had shut off the waterworks and was dealing with the pain nicely.

"'ot 'oo 'ad e i 'on 'ite ow," answered Peter.

"You got it good," said Kurt, admiring Peter's wound. "Look what I got."

Kurt stuck his finger out, like he was pointing at Peter's nose. Peter leaned forward to inspect the damage. Most of Kurt's fingers on his right hand were red and blistering, but his index finger had been uniquely burned. Branded into the tip was an instantly recognizable profile of Her Majesty, Queen Elizabeth.

"'ool!" observed Peter, genuinely impressed.

• • •

"Trick or treat!" exclaimed the happy collection of boys and girls who had been making the rounds together for nearly an hour and were already weighed down with sacks of sweets.

Agnes Worthington had to hurry to get her treats out of the oven where they had been baking for the last twenty minutes at 360 degrees, just like her favourite brownie recipe. She threw her "kiss the cook" apron over her head and peeked inside with her thick bifocals, satisfying herself that her latest creation was quite done.

"Help yourselves, children," replied Mrs. Worthington, as she returned to the front door and held out the cookie tray in her oven-gloved hands.

The children dug in greedily. No one questioned why the cookie tray, fresh from the oven, held no cookies, chocolate chip or otherwise. Instead, the tray was brimming with a generous helping of pennies, shiny and new.

And piping hot.

Kurt McGowan, at the head of the group, was the first to start screaming once it was too late and his fingers were already buried up to the second knuckle. Most of the others were able to withdraw after an initial touch that sent a sharp searing signal of pain straight to their brains, warning of an ambush and not the generous UNICEF donation they had expected.

"Serves you right, you little bastards!" Mrs. Worthington screeched at the fleeing cowboys and astronauts, ballerinas and Raggedy Annes. "Little bastards!"

She wanted to curse out the horrid creatures some more, but Mrs. Worthington's lungs were old and her voice hoarse. She knew she couldn't project like she used to, back when she was a young mother and had first come to realize she secretly hated children—and not just the little coloured ones, either. Instead, Mrs. Worthington was forced to retire back into her home, to watch some more television and return the cookie tray of pennies to the oven in anticipation of the next group of candy beggars.

● ● ●

"At least it wasn't razor blades in the apples like Mr. Hayes on 12th."

This observation came from eleven-year-old Scotty Elmont who was, everyone agreed, the coolest kid at school. Kurt considered Scotty his number one best friend, but then so did a dozen other boys and one or two tomboys.

Scotty was neither sick nor injured, but was stuck in the emergency room just the same. His younger brother, Theo, was in anaphylactic shock after taking a bite of a peanut-laden candy bar. Their single dad had piled both boys in the car and rushed them over to the hospital within moments of Theo hitting the floor. Theo was now in a coma, which concerned no one. This sort of thing happened at least once, usually twice a year, and Theo had always fully recovered within a few days. Everyone was patiently waiting for the seven-year-old to get the picture and learn to leave the peanuts and the peanut butter and the peanut brittle well enough alone. But Theo, who was an otherwise bright young boy, seemed to have a blind spot when it came to his deadly allergy. At this point, Scotty was resigned to the idea that one day his brother would either learn or die. It was really up to him.

Peter nodded in agreement. His wound wasn't nearly as interesting as Kurt's, who could look forward to showing off his royal portrait for weeks until it began to heal over. Stitches—even stitches in his gums—wouldn't attract half the attention during recess and lunch.

"Someone ought to get Worthington back for that one," Scotty mused aloud as he picked at his stump. The spirit gum element of his favourite costume was starting to itch right at the juncture where his left arm used to be.

Scotty Elmont was never so happy to be an amputee as on Hallowe'en. He had made a custom of casting aside his prosthetic arm on that special occasion and painting his stump blood red so it would look like his missing limb had only recently been yanked off at the elbow. As he grew older, his makeup effects became more elaborate. Glue and stands of yarn did a fine job of simulating dangling ligaments and arteries, and when he was feeling extra ambitious, he'd affix an old ham bone to the tip of his truncated arm to simulate a humerus jutting out the end of a fresh wound. Once he felt he was sufficiently gory, he'd roam the streets trying to solicit handshakes from horrified passersby.

Without his artificial limb, Scotty was left with only one free hand to carry his candy, making it difficult to hold the bag open to receive more loot. But it was worth the inconvenience to have the most convincing maiming of any of the boys who revelled in walking around with fake axes buried in their heads, or ping-pong eyeballs popping out of their sockets. One year a young thalidomide victim had come to town, and Scotty was concerned he would have some stiff competition that Hallowe'en. The boy had no arms—just two flipper hands jutting out of his shoulders. Scotty saw the endless costume possibilities and was troubled. However, the thalidomide kid opted not to take advantage of his physical deformity, and made the trick-or-treating rounds in a disappointing hobo getup. Scotty reigned supreme for another year, but he was still glad when his only potential rival moved to another school district the following spring.

"Worthington and Hayes both," suggested Hugh Winburn as he came over to join the discussion.

"Nah. Hayes is harmless," concluded Alan Jaycox, who didn't want to be left out.

"You call tricking a kid into eating a razor harmless?" said Kurt, who felt obliged to speak for Peter since he could barely talk.

"He's nuts. Everyone knows to skip his house," Alan elaborated.

"Razor blades in apples are pretty mean, but you'd have to be a sucker to fall for that one," declared Scotty, who then added, "No offence, Pete."

"'un 'aken," replied Peter.

"Red-hot pennies, though. That's the product of a sick mind."

Everyone nodded silently, agreeing with Scotty's assessment.

"I think she's a witch," declared Kurt with such conviction, the other boys had to wonder if he was serious.

"What makes you think so?" asked Hugh.

"Because it's Hallowe'en, dummy."

And that reason seemed to satisfy everyone.

Scotty was the first to speak after several moments of contemplative silence.

"Well you know what they do to witches, don't you?"

• • •

Neil was just dismissing Todd Anderson, who tonight had graduated from chronic bed wetting to three stitches behind his left ear. The cause of the bed wetting was still a mystery, but the stitches were the results of a high-sticking incident with a trick-or-treater dressed as a favourite NHL goalie. Todd was supposed to be a vampire, but looked more like a spaceman. So many reflective safety strips covered his costume he could very nearly be seen from orbit. He insisted the hockey stick to the head had been a failed attempt to stake him for walking the earth as one of the undead. Neil suspected it had more to do with Todd's annoying habit of whistling when he breathed.

Neil was joined by a couple of residents who had just unloaded their own patients. According to the pecking order, Neil had first pick of any interesting cases on hand. Nothing really struck his fancy, but he found himself focusing on Peter. Peter was still wearing the rubber cowl from his costume since it couldn't be removed without jostling the protruding razor blade. Neil decided it provided an interesting complication to a procedure that might not otherwise keep him awake for the next ten minutes.

"I'll take Batman," he announced, and left the two residents to fight over his leftovers.

Peter's mother came to lead her son away from his roundtable meeting with the other neighbour-hood boys. He was reluctant to leave his friends, and even more reluctant to face the razor extraction, but the original focus of the discussion had already come to its conclusion. The beginnings of a plot had been formed, and now the topic of conversation had switched to more pressing points of debate like comic books and sports cards.

• • •

Traditionally speaking, if you knock on a door and don't get a treat, you're supposed to deliver your trick in a reasonable amount of time. On or near Hallowe'en is accepted protocol. The boys didn't understand that there was a statute of limitations on Hallowe'en tricks, so their revenge was plotted for Christmas. The intervening weeks were used to heal their wounds and come up with something audacious. It was Scotty, having survived the night unscathed, who did most of the legwork in preparation for D-day. This involved nearly nightly trips to Mrs. Worthington's house under cover of darkness with a file and a can of lighter fluid.

The police had stopped by once to respond to complaints about Agnes Worthington's nasty Hallowe'en prank that had hurt a couple dozen children— none too seriously. They ultimately decided not to press charges, even after she accused the officers of being agents of Satan and threatened to turn the garden hose on them. Mrs. Worthington was the sort of neighbour who inspired plenty of complaints, but none so serious as to require a court appearance. City prosecutors wanted no part of seeking fines or jail time for the petty crimes of a woman who looked like everyone's favourite aunt or grandmother, especially when any accusations could be countered with claims of senility or mental illness. They once tried to pin a series of cat poisonings on her, but abandoned that idea due to lack of evidence. The oven-roasted pennies incident had been her most serious infraction since the last of six cats had vomited and died within a hundred yards of her house years earlier. Perhaps things might have turned out better for all involved if the justice system had pursued retribution this time around, but once again the police and prosecutors decided to leave well enough alone.

One of the most common complaints about Mrs. Worthington was her vintage Christmas lights. They were vintage through age rather than design, having been up for almost thirty consecutive years. Stringing them around the front windows of the house and over the porch's eaves trough was the last service her husband had performed for her before he finally packed up their children and left her for a woman half her age and twice as hateful. Her neighbours were fed up with looking at them year round, and few could deny that a string of Christmas lights stopped being festive by March. A proposed city ordinance addressing the tardy removal of Christmas decorations was bogged down in bureaucracy, but remained alive due, in part, to the three-decade-and-counting run of the Worthington lights.

It was the Christmas lights that drew Scotty's attention during his nightly trespasses. The whole neighbourhood knew from experience that Mrs. Worthington plugged in her Christmas lights exactly once a year for about twenty-four hours, from Christmas Eve to Christmas night. Then they went off again for another year. Scotty saw a window of opportunity for vengeance and was determined to seize it.

The rest of the boys, for their part, limited themselves to acting as Scotty's personal cheering section, urging him on, assuring him that this was a brilliant idea that would go off without a hitch, but closely guarding their plausible deniability should things go badly. Sneaking onto Mrs. Worthington's porch each night, Scotty would cup one of the colourful Christmas bulbs in the blunt double-pronged hook of his prosthetic arm and then patiently saw away at a small section of the glass with the iron file he had liberated from under his father's work bench. Once he had ground enough of the thin glass shell away to make a small hole, he would poke the nozzle of his can of lighter fluid into the bulb and fill it until the liquid touched the tip of the filament inside. He would then repeat this procedure on the next Christmas light in line. It was highly delicate work, but years of model-aircraft construction had given Scotty a light touch, and he broke only two bulbs outright, and slightly cracked another three.

Each night, Scotty would try to work through at least six bulbs, averaging ten, and managing as many as twenty on one particularly productive evening. By the time the sun had risen on the morning of Christmas Eve, Scotty had successfully sabotaged over four hundred individual lights all across Mrs. Worthington's front porch, from the eves, down the support posts, and woven through the slatted wooden rails on the deck. He never managed to get to all of them, but he figured his ambitious project had accounted for over seventy-five percent of the entire daisy-chain.

Getting out of the house after dark on Christmas Eve was a simple matter for all the boys in on the scheme. They had planted the seed of an excuse weeks earlier, claiming an organized carolling excursion which, all the parents agreed, sounded absolutely adorable. Many of the parents wanted to come along and take pictures for the family album, but each of the boys was armed with the same plea for their moms and dads to please not embarrass them in front of their school buddies. They promised there would be ample photo ops when the group eventually came around to their own house to offer something fairly traditional and reasonably on-key. Of course, there was no intention to ever utter a single seasonal note. If the carollers were questioned about being no-shows, the agreed-upon story was that they had all gotten cold after working the first couple of blocks and accepted one neighbour's invitation inside for a round of hot chocolate. Time, they would claim, just slipped away after that.

The first few kids gathered outside the Worthington house late in the afternoon, a good hour before sunset. Nobody wanted to miss the fireworks, and there was no set time for the lights to turn on. Sometime after dark was the closest anyone could estimate. Word had spread throughout the entire school about the impending spectacle, and by the time the crisp winter sky lit up red with a breathtaking sunset no one had the slightest interest in looking at, the street in front of Mrs. Worthington's bungalow was packed with a playground's-worth of children.

About half an hour after the sun dipped under the horizon of rooftops and the streetlights all came on, the main event started without any fanfare or warning. Somewhere in the house, a plug had been pushed into an electrical socket, sparking hundreds of light bulb filaments right over hundreds of tiny reservoirs of lighter fluid. It happened with such a complete lack of warning, only a handful of the audience happened to be looking directly at the Worthington house at the moment of ignition. What they saw was the string of lights exploding in a line of white flashes that dripped blazing dollops of lighter fluid into the hedges. Glass shrapnel from the bulbs made it as far as the curb, but none of the observers was hit.

After an initial group-gasp reaction from the crowd, there was a smattering of laughter and a few isolated pockets of applause. The commotion died down quickly, and the first couple of minutes following the initial bang were anticlimactic. The flames licked at the house's aluminium siding and brick walls, failing to get a foothold. The porch was a wood structure, however, and the edges of the roof flickered with a low flame that struggled for survival against the damp wood. Just when it looked like the disappointing blaze would burn out all by itself, large plumes of smoke started to rise from between the shingles. The flames had managed to worm their way under the roof and find plenty of dry timber in the rafters of the attic crawlspace. As the entire roof started to catch, it seemed this would be a reasonably spectacular inferno after all. The audience looked on quietly, content in the assumption that one of the neighbours would notice and call the fire department.

The emergency-room conspirators watched the fire spread, unsure if this had been the ultimate plan all along, afraid to say anything just in case they were the only one in the group who had thought this was supposed to begin and end with the destruction of some universally loathed Christmas lights. From a safe distance, they examined the Worthington house for any sign of life or movement.

"Jeezuz," said Alan, who had been warned repeatedly against using the Lord's name in vain around the holidays and avoided this sin through mispronunciation, "That's Scotty in there!"

Sure enough, standing in the centre of the living room window, poking through Mrs. Worthington's drab off-white curtains, was Scotty, waving both his stump and his one good arm at them frantically. He wasn't wearing his prosthetic limb, but where he may have misplaced it seemed to be the least of Scotty's worries at the moment. There was mortal panic written all over his face.

● ● ●

Scotty had woken up early on December 24th after a poor night's sleep. Something was nagging at him, but he was at a loss to pinpoint exactly what. He ate little at breakfast with his brother, and was so distracted he almost neglected to discourage Theo from spreading peanut butter on his toast. It was nearly lunch by the time Scotty pinpointed the source of his nagging concern—what he had done to the Worthington house. It wasn't that his petty act of vandalism might ultimately escalate into full-scale arson, but rather that his weeks of effort might all come to naught. He remembered the last time he had employed his father's favourite brand-name lighter fluid, when he used half a can to burn out a prodigious ant hill. The leftovers had evaporated by the time some stubborn charcoal briquettes needed to be helped along. Barbeques were uncommon at the Elmont homestead, and months had passed before Scotty's father discovered his son had left the cap off. Now Scotty found himself wondering how many of his sabotaged Christmas bulbs may have gone dry since he first began his project.

That afternoon, Scotty decided to swing by the Worthington house with his can of lighter fluid to make sure the evening's show would be every bit as spectacular as he'd originally envisioned. Although there remained enough lighter fluid collected at the bottom of each bulb to assure near-total destruction of the entire string of lights, some of the earliest filed and filled bulbs were running low. Scotty had never intruded on the Worthington property by the light of day, but he decided to risk it this one time in order to top off a dozen or so bulbs he thought needed a full tank of fuel to explode with maximum effect.

Scotty never heard Mrs. Worthington approach. He felt her first—specifically her gnarled fingernails, thick with many layers of nail polish, digging into his flesh as she grabbed him by the rim of his ear and pulled him inside her house. There was nobody on the street to catch Scotty's cry of protest, and once the door slammed shut behind him, any chance of someone hearing was extinguished.

Mrs. Worthington turned the latch on the door and proceeded to drag Scotty down the hall and into her kitchen. He didn't dare struggle for fear of splitting his ear open on her claws.

"I don't care for children snooping around my property. I don't care for children at all, but children on my property get under my skin. I'd sic the dogs on you if I kept any of the filthy beasts. What are you doing here and don't give me lies!"

Mrs. Worthington released Scotty and stared him down, waiting for an answer. Scotty couldn't think of any reasonable explanation for his presence, so he simply said the first thing that came to mind. As it happened, it was closer to the truth than he'd ever intended to get, not that Mrs. Worthington recognized or appreciated it.

"Trick or treat?"

Mrs. Worthington looked Scotty up and down for a long time.

"Boy, are you stupid in the head?" she said.

Scotty wasn't sure what to say. He certainly felt stupid for being nabbed so easily.

"Seems brains aren't all you're missing. How'd you lose that?" asked Mrs. Worthington, pointing her chin at Scotty's artificial limb. "Horsing around where you shouldn't have, I'd say."

"I guess so," Scotty agreed, glad to avoid recounting a more detailed history.

Mrs. Worthington grabbed Scotty by the shoulders and spun him around so his back was facing her. Pulling down the collar of his coat, exposing some bare neck, she reached for a large pair of scissors that hung from a hook that was hammered into the faded pot-and-kettle wallpaper of her kitchen. Scotty felt the cold metal of the scissor blades slide across the back of his shirt before slipping under one of the leather straps that held his prosthetic arm in place. One forceful snip later and Mrs. Worthington was through the strap. The limb came free and dangled loosely. With a sharp tug on the hook end of Scotty's arm, Mrs. Worthington yanked it out of the sleeve of his coat.

"Hey! Give it back!" Scotty protested.

Mrs. Worthington tossed the limb onto the top of her refrigerator with a careless backhanded fling. It landed at the rear of the greasy appliance surface, well out of reach of the boy who was still a few years away from achieving his full height.

"You'll get it back when I'm satisfied with the job you've done."

"What job?" Scotty asked, not even trying to mask his suspicious dread.

"The job that makes amends for your snooping around and horsing around and whatnot."

● ● ●

"Scotty!" Kurt yelled through the thick oak wood, "Unlock the door!"

Of his stunned and amazed friends, Kurt was the only one who ran to the Worthington house to help.

"I can't!" Scotty yelled back.

Unlocking the door from the inside meant turning a latch and the door knob at the same time. Two hands were required to accomplish this and, despite his best efforts, Scotty soon discovered that one hand and a stump simply weren't up to the task. After two solid hours of toil, he still hadn't earned his arm back. Not to Mrs. Worthington's satisfaction.

The job Scotty had been unwillingly recruited for would haunt him for the rest of his days. Pulling Mrs. Worthington's oven out from the wall had merely been backbreaking. Scrubbing the floor underneath it was both backbreaking and horrifying. The linoleum was coated in decades of spillage and dust that had turned black as it developed the consistency of tar. Scotty had to fight his gag reflex as he scraped at it with soapy water and a stiff brush, especially when he spotted something that he could actually identify as food. A single dry noodle or fossilized pea was somehow even more sickening than the sea of filth they came to be stuck in. A routine of scrubbing and soaking, scrubbing and soaking set in and Scotty lost all track of time. He didn't even realize night had fallen when Mrs. Worthington grunted and raised herself out of her ratty recliner one final time, tearing herself away from her television stories. He thought she was coming to check on his progress and criticize his work ethic again, but she turned left instead of right when she hit the hall. He couldn't imagine what she was up to until he heard her wheezing as she bent down to push a plug into a spare socket. Scotty wasted a critical moment deciding whether he should shout "Wait!" "Stop!" or "Don't!"—not that a single word of warning would have done a thing to discourage Mrs. Worthington from turning on her Christmas lights.

"What about the back door?" Kurt suggested.

"I already tried! It's no good!" The back door lock had been an even more complex mix of latches and knobs. Scotty was unsure how Mrs. Worthington ever got it open without three hands.

"Can you open a window?"

"I'll try."

Scotty retreated back into the burning building that was starting to fill with smoke. All the windows he'd seen so far had been painted shut. He figured it was about time to find something he could use to break one. It had to be hefty enough to smash the glass and knock out all the shards around the edges, but light enough that Scotty could pick it up and swing it with one hand. Nothing in the immediate vicinity fit the bill and the thickening smoke was reducing visibility quickly, making it harder to find something suitable with every passing moment.

Scotty could hear Mrs. Worthington hacking somewhere in the house, lost in dense fumes. She roared with a smoker's cough that was earned years before her house started burning all around her. Even as the roof began to cave in with a tremendous crash of splitting beams, Mrs. Worthington's fearsome cough was the loudest noise Scotty could hear. It sounded like an evil chortle, punctuated by a distinct chanting whisper, "Little bastard, little bastard, where have you got to?"

Scotty was certain if she got her claws into him again, she wouldn't let go. Mrs. Worthington would hold on tight until the whole house burned to the ground and all they would ever find of him would be the metal hook of his lost arm.

Outside, Kurt was determined to keep up his end of the rescue. He ran through the crunching remains of hundreds of burst Christmas lights, looking for an alternate exit for Scotty. His eyes fell on a basement window, poking up above the snow line. Kurt pressed his face to the glass and cupped his hands around his eyes, peering inside. The latch was open, but he could see nothing but black beyond the window frame. It took nearly a full minute of pushing at the top and scratching at the base to pry the window open— plenty of time for the fire to spread from the attic to the ground floor.

Kurt poked his head through the window and looked around as his eyes adjusted to the dark. The basement was nothing but open walls and storage space. Boxes were piled high, all the way up to the open window, and Kurt figured they could be scaled easily provided they were full of non-breakables. He swung a leg inside and put some weight on the top box, testing it to make sure it offered a solid foothold. It did, right up until Kurt slipped and fell. The entire pile of boxes held strong, making his tumble into the basement that much more bruise-inducing. He landed face-down on the concrete floor and felt the cool stone on his cheek. It took him a moment to regain his senses and remember there was a very hot inferno consuming everything in its path just one floor above.

Kurt picked himself up and started shouting, "Scotty! Get to the basement! I found a way out!"

Kurt could hear Scotty's heavy footfalls above his head as his friend searched for the door to the basement. Kurt looked around, too scared to venture farther inside, not quite ready to retreat back out the window. This was the lair local kids speculated about, often wildly, never accurately. Disappointingly, it looked like any other unfinished basement Kurt had seen in his life, with a bare floor and walls made mostly of wooden cross beams and supports. The only difference was the amount of clutter—unhappy decades' worth, piled on memories best forgotten. Kurt was calculating the age of some of the furniture based on the coats of dust when he spotted...*it*.

There, sitting on one cross beam, deep in the recess of an exposed wall, was a pickle jar filled to the rim with a fortune in pennies. Long since cooled after the end of the Hallowe'en festivities, they waited patiently for their next trip to the oven and the inevitable visit from greedy trick-or-treaters. Or at least for the next time Mrs. Worthington bothered to roll them and bring them to the bank.

"Treasure," Kurt said aloud under his breath. "Witch treasure."

Distracted by the allure of the Hallowe'en bounty he'd been denied nearly two months earlier, Kurt found himself reaching into the secret hiding place he'd discovered. It would only take a moment to snatch his prize, and then Kurt would be able to spend the holidays rattling his penny jar at his friends and bragging about the treasure he'd captured from the very bowels of the witch's den. He was pretty sure pennies didn't count as real theft and wouldn't result in criminal charges, or worse, a grounding.

Digging deep, his arm buried into the recess of the wall up to his shoulder, Kurt was just able to touch the penny jar with the tips of his fingers. He stretched, trying to hook the jar lid with his fingernails. Instead of finding the grip he was looking for, Kurt only managed to push the jar off the far edge of the wooden beam it was perched on. The penny jar plummeted to the concrete floor and shattered, sending its fortune scattering in all directions. What he thought had been a secret hiding place had actually been an obscured view of the open space on the other side.

Kurt started to withdraw his arm until he felt a terrible stabbing pain in his forearm. The pain was so sharp and unexpected, it took a moment for him to realize it was actually several terrible stabbing pains all at once. He winced, but held his screams to himself. With that old witch Worthington upstairs somewhere, Scotty in need of rescue, and the whole house in flames, now didn't seem like the time to add to the chaos with a bunch of panicked yelling and hollering, even when his arm hurt more than anything ever.

Kurt ducked his head down to look into the hole in the wall and see what it was that had grabbed onto his arm like a mouthful of shark teeth. Jutting from various cross beams inside, Kurt could see a number of nails sticking out. They had all been hastily bent and hammered down by the construction workers who had built the house a million years ago. Angled away from where Kurt stood, he had been able to worm his arm past them unharmed. But now that he was trying to pull back out, the nail tips were hooked under his skin in several spots. A few of them looked deep, all looked rusty.

That was bound to earn a tetanus booster shot, thought Kurt.

He tried to pull his arm free, but that only made the rusty nails dig further under his skin. The pain shot all the way up his arm and into his head, bouncing around inside his skull like ricocheting bullets. He was sure if he pulled any harder, the nails would peel the flesh off his whole arm like an elbow-length glove.

"What are you standing around for? We gotta go!"

Scotty had finally found the route to the basement and was now standing impatiently at Kurt's side, tugging at his coat with his one hand, prodding him towards the open window with his stump.

"I'm stuck!" Kurt protested against Scotty's persistent jostling.

"How stuck?"

Scotty didn't wait for the details. He ducked his head and had a look down the hole where he could see the many nails chewing into Kurt's arm for himself.

"That is super-fucking stuck," Scotty concluded. "Wait here! I'll find something to get you out."

For as long as he dared, Scotty searched the basement for a tool that would help him set Kurt free. The fire upstairs was spreading quickly and licks of flame were probing through the floorboards above their heads, dropping embers into the cellar, looking for new fuel to ignite. There was plenty waiting, all of it dry and highly flammable. When Scotty finally returned to Kurt's side, he brought only one tool with him—apparently the only tool the decidedly unhandy Agnes Worthington had ever owned. It was a hatchet and it was far down Scotty's mental list of items he would have preferred to use to get the job done.

Kurt looked at the hatchet in Scotty's one good hand. It was old and spotted with corrosion, but still sharp. Kurt nodded in resignation. He could see the fear in Scotty's eyes. It told him there was no other option, and if there had been, Scotty would have seized it in an instant rather than go through with this particular plan.

Kurt closed his eyes, bracing for a pain he knew would be far worse than what he was already imagining. "Just try to get it off in one good shot."

● ● ●

It took three.

What happened after that was a blur to Scotty, who felt woozy from what he had just watched himself do, and a total blackout of memory to Kurt. With his one hand hooked under Kurt's armpit, Scotty managed to half-drag and half-carry him up the hill of old boxes and antique furniture until he was able to shove Kurt back out through the basement window.

When their friends saw the two boys scrambling out of the blazing house, a few of the braver ones ran forward to help them get clear of the building. Scotty collapsed to the ground, coughing uncontrollably, while some of the other boys slapped his back unhelpfully. Everyone was still reacting to the amount of Kurt's blood they'd managed to get all over themselves when they noticed that Kurt himself was nowhere to be seen.

"Where'd he go?" one wondered aloud.

It didn't take a great tracker to figure it out. The blood trail in the snow was obvious, leading away across Mrs. Worthington's property and into the street.

Kurt lived only a couple of blocks away. Even out of his head with pain and shock and blood loss, he was able to find his way home on autopilot, gripping his open wound tightly with his remaining hand, slowing the flow of blood just enough to keep himself alive. Kurt only let go of his pumping artery to let himself in through the front door. He stumbled through the house, tracking snow and mud and blood across his mother's nice clean floors, until he found her in the living room laying presents under the Christmas tree.

"I don't think we should wait to go to the hospital this time," he announced before collapsing.

● ● ●

The third worst shift of all was Christmas. Nobody wanted to be stuck servicing seasonal injuries during a holiday that was reserved for giving and receiving and reconnecting with family and friends. Even the Jews on the staff didn't want to get stuck with the Christmas shift, and usually spent most of December trying to negotiate for the time off. Christmas injuries and illnesses weren't as plentiful or specific as on other occasions. Mostly they amounted to the usual sort of patient complaints that come in wintertime, such as falls and collisions due to icy conditions. Come Christmas morning, however, you could always count on one or two incidents arising from novices trying out their expensive new Christmas gifts. Power tools usually.

It hadn't been a power tool that had lobbed off one boy's arm at the elbow. It had been something more primitive, like an axe. Maybe the result of a firewood chopping accident. Neil didn't ask. The mother seemed completely clueless and all the boy would say was how disappointed he was that he had to lose the one with his unique Queen Elizabeth brand. It was the painkillers talking. The police could fish for more details if they were interested. For his part, Neil was done with the triage and was satisfied the kid was stable enough to be sent upstairs for more stitches and a transfusion. Right now he was stuck dealing with some crazy old lady with smoke inhalation on top of a four-pack-a-day cough. She'd been found wandering the streets without proper winter attire and making little to no sense. What clothes she wore were blackened and burned in places, but otherwise she seemed to have survived her ordeal—whatever it may have been—perfectly intact. It was a Christmas miracle. Physically she seemed fine.

"Go straight to hell you bastard," the old lady told Neil when he first approached her to make his basic assessment.

Mentally it was another matter. The old lady hacked violently and spat some sooty phlegm in Neil's face. She cackled, amused at her own proficient aim. Social services would be called and she would quickly and efficiently be filed away into the system. The sooner the better. Neil still felt bad about some of the hard-luck cases that passed through his emergency room. Others he couldn't wait to be rid of, Christmas miracle or not.

"Hey, Neil. Congrats on the trifecta," one senior resident called out in passing.

"What are you talking about?"

"They just posted the schedule for next week. Guess who pulled the New Year's Eve shift."

• • •

Scotty never went trick or treating as the one-armed boy again. Somehow it didn't seem as amusing as it once did. Come the next Hallowe'en, he teamed up with Kurt and they went out as the two-headed monster. Kurt supplied the left arm, Scotty the right. Both boys performed one head each.

Of his dozen potential best friends, Scotty had finally settled on one.

About the Author

Shane Simmons is an award-winning screenwriter and graphic novelist whose work has appeared in international film festivals, museums and lectures about design and structure. His art has been discussed in multiple books and academic journals about sequential storytelling, and his short stories have been printed in critically praised anthologies of history, crime and horror. He lives in Montreal with his wife and too many cats.

Also by Shane Simmons

Novels

Filmography
Sex Tape

Collections

Raw and Other Stories

Booklets

Carrion Luggage
Choke the Chicken
The Red Baron: An Ace for the Ages

Graphic Novels

The Long and Unlearned Life of Roland Gethers
The Failed Promise of Bradley Gethers
The Inauspicious Adventures of Filson Gethers

Last Words

Small-press publishers rely on reviews from readers like you to help get the word out about their books. Whether it's a simple star rating or a written critique, every bit of feedback helps convince the impersonal computer algorithms of Amazon, and other literary outlets, that the book you just read has merit and deserves more exposure. Please support independent authors, editors and publishers by taking a few moments to share your thoughts and opinions with other potential readers who may be sitting on the fence about trying an intriguing novel or collection. Your suggestions or comments can make all the difference when it comes to helping them find a new writer they'll like, or matching a struggling author with the readership he or she deserves. Thank you.

www.ingramcontent.com/pod-product-compliance
Lightning Source LLC
Chambersburg PA
CBHW020610130626
46552CB00007B/3131